INFLAME

An intriguing romance story

The restaurant was calm now; most of the people had left. The tables had dirty dishes lying on them and a lot of dirty leftovers were strewn around the tables.

Angelina finished entering the last record for the day in the small computer the manager insisted she used. When she saw that the numbers in her notepad added up to the same amount the screen displayed, she knew she had successfully made the day through without an error.

"Are you done with the accounts?" a masculine voice inquired beside her.

"Yes sir," she responded, feeling that annoying fear she felt at the manager's presence.

"Oh. Beautiful," he observed, staring quickly at the final figures on the screen. Benjamin seemed pleased.

He was always pleased when the records were straight and intact and didn't require his presence. The only other day he wasn't pleased was when he had to pay the workers' wages. "So, clear the dishes and you can get going."

"Thanks, sir." Angelina walked back to the main section of their restaurant. Some of the dishes had been cleared by the time she got there. Angelina was shocked.

While she was still standing, wondering which of the other workers had been grateful enough to do the generous task, she saw her target at the end of the hall collecting the last set of dishes.

"Hello?" He said with a beaming smile.

"It's you!" she screamed out of excitement. The excitement didn't stem from happiness at seeing him but from the pleasure of his relieving deed.

Some minutes after, she was sitting beside the helper in his car.

"Frankly, I didn't think that you would finally accept to take a ride with me."

"It's been two weeks," she replied, "And what you did tonight was very touching."

He smiled at himself, pleased at his deed. "If I didn't consider the fact that you are exhausted already, I'd have said we go out on a date tonight."

She smiled, "Maybe not so fast, but surely, I shall accept to go on a date with you soon."

He was pleased, "I'd hold my breath."

Bob licked his lips as Angelina walked into her apartment.

The first time he met her, it was at the restaurant, where he had driven there to take a bite. She had served him in such a polite manner on that day. Her gesture had left him wondering how a beautiful lady like Angelina still had the capacity to respect people; despite the challenge, she would have been experiencing with tons of men trying desperately to woo her heart.

'She'd be mine soon.' Bob told himself as he relished the sweet snacks with even greater hunger.

When he asked for her name, she threw her curtsey away for the moment.

"Kindly stick to the diet you came here for." She said, slipping past him to attend to a fresh customer with a happy face.

Her face, when she spoke to him, momentarily became more beautiful at the disappearance of curtsey.

"Just tell me your name." He'd insisted when he was

about leaving. And seeing that they both knew the obvious, he concluded by saying; "I'd call you Angel'Lina"

Her name was inscribed on her tag, but he chose to pretend like he could not see it earlier, simply because he wanted her to say it through her small cute lips.

Angelina wasn't going to fall prey to such anymore.

Bob

The heater wasn't on, but the two figures on the bed were sweltering from the heat of their copulation. Bob looked again at the windows to ensure that they were widely opened to the air outside.

The fresh breeze could only do little to the intensity of

their movements. It wasn't over yet; Bob took his mind off the challenge of aeration and grabbed the lady's waist to turn her over. He loved the way she submitted to his commands; making the moves the instant he tapped her.

Now he intended to give her doggy style. He could see her knowing smile as she bent over to receive him right into her steamy spot.

Angelina was exceptional because her emotions were not easily hidden in her sweet looks. She had a lovely brow that creased quickly to show all the emotions she was going through.

Before proceeding into his next action, Bob tilted her head toward him, while he bent his head into an arc for another taste of her lips. The down-curve of it was moist and it sucked on him too as though she wanted to drain him of all the fluids he had.

Her soul was pleased, that much he could tell from the small display her eyes revealed when it fluttered as he let her head return to a comfortable state.

As he smashed her from behind with movements that marveled him, he loved the groans and the moans and the scream for more. But most of all, he loved the way she shuddered at his touch.

"I love this." He whispered in her ears.

"Oh baby!" she moaned.

Imaginations of her hard face, the first time he met her at the restaurant played through his mind. Who would have believed that such a brave girl would soon be wiggling her butt beneath him, and screaming like a child? The thoughts alone would feed him pleasantly in the following days.

This was a wish that had become a reality. And once again, the gamer smiled at just how he could get any lady he laid his plans on.

When the session was finally over, he moaned very loudly and crashed on the bed beside her.

The room was thick with the acrid smell and taste of their copulation. He ran his hand restlessly on her stomach, enjoying the way she twitched like an electric current as he drew circles with seeds he had spilled on her.

"Promise me," she said silently, through a face beaming with all the life of a very wonderfully enjoyed moment, "that you will love me forever."

"I said that earlier, Angel'Lina. I'd love you till eternity."

Angelina thought about what it was to have this sweet

moment forever. It wasn't a dream for her anymore. With the promising man lying exhaustedly across her and playing his hands over her, it had become a dream come true.

-

The following morning, Bob left the hotel quite early. The pleasures of the previous day had now washed off his face. He took his phone and checked his chat.

Hey, Loverboy! Where have you been all day? You've rendered me restless since last night.
Call me when you see this. Xoxo.

Bob's face beamed with a smile. Finally, he had triggered just what he wanted to hear out of his next target.

He clothed himself quickly and left the hotel before Angelina woke from the bed.

"You can see that I have two beautiful daughters right?" Julia inquired from the man sitting close to her.

They were sitting together by sheer coincidence, in the spectators' seats of the Lions Basketball court, where they were both cheering the Lions in their home match against the Fierce Bulls of DC.

Julia knew she was beautiful, but she couldn't read how the man beside her was able to see through her ocean of helpless loneliness. As the man stared at her, however, he seemed to be seeing that all the beauty of the universe could not compete with the face he was staring at.

She always wondered why men felt very desperate to be friends with her. When she was pregnant with Sharon, one man had been so obsessed with her restless gold hair, that he insisted he'd pay anything just to be with her. She had laughed it off, choosing to think that he was insane for desiring to get laid by a heavily pregnant woman.

"I see that." The man responded with a cheeky grin.

"But if you would allow me, I'd like to show you that I can care for you and your children."

"My mom does not need your care!" barked the little girl. It was as she spoke that Julia noticed that she shouldn't have allowed the discussion to continue when she knew her daughter was listening.

"Hey, Sarah, stop that, don't be mean." She cautioned. Julia wasn't going to allow her daughter to take advantage of the moment to explore her insolent tendencies.

With the young man's insistence, Julia and her daughter

were walking to the park by him and he offered Julia his business card.

"I'd be dying to see your call." He insisted and winked.

Even if she took her mind off everything else, it was hard to ignore that charming wink on his face when he dispersed. It was an expert way of registering his naughty sides in the manner Julia thought about when she felt hungry for a man's touch.

Days after, she was rolling over her bed, staring angrily at the business card with his number winking at her in the same manner that he had done to her also.

Just give me a chance! The card screamed in her head. She remembered how his face sparked with passion like orbs of fierce fire.

Julia grabbed her phone and dialed his number.

"Hello, Bob." She said as he picked on the second ring.

"Julia!"

Julia didn't expect that a man that charmed with a single sight would remember her voice in an instant.

Some hours later, he parked outside her garage and walked his 6.5fts into her apartment.

Tall men had always struck her; she remembered that much as he bent through her doorway. By the time he arrived, she had momentarily overcome the passion that had driven her to call him over.

"Mommy, who is this man?" Sharon inquired.

The man wore a friendly smile.

"Sharon dear. Bob is my friend. He was at your game last Friday."

"Really?" Sharon responded.

"I don't like him, mommy." Julia's little girl said.

"No Sarah, Bob is our friend." She responded. "and kindly speak respectfully to strangers."

After eating with the family, She pleaded with him to stay the night. She didn't need to plead for too long, it was what he too desired.

"Bob," she said firmly. It was hard for him to stay decent while she was clad in her irresistible translucent gown. His eyes bored through the gown to trace out her nipple. "Please listen to me."

"I'm listening," he said briefly, but soon drifted his eyes to his initial focus.

Julia chose to ignore him; "I have been through this before, and I don't want to go ahead anymore if this is not going to be something serious."

"I promise you," he said sternly, "I would always love and care for you." He declared.

She could only resort to faith since she had spent the earlier moment with him telling him about the calamitous outcome of her past relationship.

While she gave him an account of her emotional encounters, he had listened attentively, interjecting with cusses on the bastards that had treated her unfairly. She hoped he was of a better breed.

Bob slowly let the line across her shoulder fall off, putting her enormous breasts before his very sight. Her nipples were stiff already; the mere sight of them aroused movement within his flies.

Soon, he had her moaning a little too loudly for a house

with kids in it. She didn't care. It was the first time since her ex's dismissal that she was receiving carnal pleasures.

Bob pushed himself into her with a force that seemed never to come out of her anymore, but before the pleasure of his entrance lingered for too long, he dragged himself near the walls of her privates and rammed in again.

She enjoyed every movement of him against her. They seemed to be dancing to the same rhythmic music that wasn't playing in reality. From time to time, Bob played his hands across her nipples like a spectrum to a guitar string. The soft feeling kept Julia horny through the entire process.

To his surprise, she came down on him and had his cock in her lips as he fired goo out of himself. He would always remember this experience.

"Never forget your promise, Bob. I am a hard woman to upset," she said playfully, enjoying the sight of him from a sweaty beardy chin, while his tummy rose and fell with exhaustion. "I know the way with men and promises, most times they fail."

He smiled and grunted, "Not all men are beasts."

She smiled too; she liked his sweet and promising comeback.

Renee

Two messages chimed in her phone.

Renee looked at it quickly and smiled.

HTG, what've u bn up 2?

And

I op our plans 2 meet 2night is still on?
She smiled at both messages. She knew she had stressed

the young man long enough and she was on the verge of

exhausting him of all the masculine strength he had in

him. He had even stuck with calling her HTG which he

told her - upon her request - was the acronym for; Hard

To Get.

It was the fifth time they would plan a date that wouldn't

materialize, no thanks to her, but Renee didn't mind.

Other men would have backed away, not Bob. She liked

his insistence, and finally, she had concluded to meet with

him.

She knew she had to prepare herself for the ordeal of

meeting him. A man that had been denied for that long

would surely come at her with a hungry urge. She needed

to be prepared.

"Please come tonight. I shall be waiting." He said in a voice message. She listened again and again to his baritone voice. She preferred voice messages from him than chats.

He always seemed to forget the fact that she was a teacher who liked people writing their expressions in its full forms, the way he shortened the texts looked almost like an insult to the person who was reading.

She had expressed her idea about the chat messages very subtly, choosing rather lead by example. When they met in person, she was planning on telling him that.

He rang her again at six, to remind her that eight o'clock was the time they'd fixed.

"Honey, if you can't make coming over, you may tell -"

"I'd be there." She cut in politely.

He hung up and anticipated this meeting. In their earlier dates, she always informed him before the time that she couldn't make coming. The fact that she didn't say anything about not coming at a close hour like six meant she was in for business.

-

Bob checked his wristwatch just in time to see seven fifty-nine turns into six. He exhaled. For some reason, he was sure this was his final bus-stop over women's issues. He had had enough of them anyway, and now that the toughest of them all was agreeing to a date with him, he was looking forward to an opportunity to propose to her in a short time.

Bob knew he might need to leave the city; too many women probably had something against him around here.

And if the priest asked the witnesses on the day of his wedding; whether or not there was anyone who didn't want the wedding to take place, Bob knew several women might. He was therefore certain that he and his newfound love would travel out of the city to wed.

As his gaze returned to the door from his watch, it was the glorious appearance of Renee that he saw scanning the room.

In the pictures and their video chats, she had seemed quite tall and big; a character that seemed like the only flaw in her entirety. As she located him and covered the strides between them, he realized that she wasn't more than a 5ft5 and her body had the perfect shape of figure 8. She walked with an elegance that commanded stares, her hair was elegantly done too; it would have qualified her for a Miss. World contest.

If Bob had the rings on him, he would surely have
proposed to her that very night.

"You look amazing?" He confessed.

"Thanks," she said with a smile.

Inferno

Bob ran a finger through Renee's skirt. His heartbeat
pounded against his chest as his hands moved gradually
and tentatively over her blouse too.

The first button came off easily.

"Go ahead" she whispered.

The softness in her voice stirred him. He loved her for
everything that she is, and now that she was handing him
the permission to explore her body, he found himself

drowning deeper in the pool of emotional and sexual satisfaction.

Soon the blouse dropped past her elbows and breasts and she allowed it to glide away from her toes.

There she was standing before his naked body and allowing him to bury his head in the space between her legs.

As his tongue rolled along with her privates, she moaned softly and grabbed the back of his head tightly against herself. The pleasure within her seemed to flow with absolute comfort.

Three women broke into the room without knocking, destabilizing the coupling duo.

Renee quickly grabbed the bedsheet and drew it over her nakedness. Bob couldn't get hold of anything before one of the ladies pulled out a gun against his head.

"Bob! Who are these?" Renee screamed.

In the eyes of the women, Bob could see revenge blazing very fiercely. How the women had united against him, left him wondering.

Bob looked from Angelina to Julia and then to Stacy. They were only a few out of the other women he had tricked into bed.

The problem was just that Bob did everything it took to get the woman he wanted, but once he had had her, the woman grew old and boring in his eye, and his urge to find a new prey set in.

Now, however, karma was staring him in the face.

He wished there was a way someone would wake him from this nightmare.

The loud bang of a shot rendered the entire room dark.

THE END